A Mother's Silent Cry

CATHY HOLMES

Order this book online at www.trafford.com
or email orders@trafford.com

Most Trafford titles are also available at major online book retailers.

Print information available on the last page.

ISBN: 978-1-4907-7303-2 (sc)
ISBN: 978-1-4907-7304-9 (e)

Trafford rev. 04/22/2016

 www.trafford.com

North America & international
toll-free: 1 888 232 4444 (USA & Canada)
fax: 812 355 4082

Acknowledgements

I give praises to God for his wonderful grace and mercy for giving me the heart he gave me, for allowing me to have a strong passion for family and people in general. And for always having a strong will to share and to give.

My loving husband Yalma for his devotion and his constant stern uphill push reminding me that he believes I can do just about anything. His strong stand by me attitude, don't worry about what people say, if they don't have any problems let them keep on living. These are some of the things in life that happen to you to test your faith, leave it in the hands of the lord.

My loving son Ernell for his encouragement his famous "quote was I know you can do it mama, you are and have always been a strong woman. I was there I watched you go through the struggles; I watched you laugh many times when you wanted to cry and hold back the tears. Always trying to make us happy in spite of what was going on.

My loving daughter Tonya for listening, laughing, and crying with me during tough times. Her inspiring statement at the ladies retreat was. "Mama I got your back, remember you made me the woman I am today by your teaching. I'm my own woman! Stay strong Mama Cathy I love you…

My loving son Lamont for his comments that has allowed me to look at things differently. Mama it's not about you it's about me in spite of the pain its causing you be strong. I thank you for not giving up on me. He has given me joy and love and I don't want to erase the good for what may have happened over the years. I have given him back to God and will continue to pray for him.

My sister Rosa for her inspiring encouragement and her never ending love, and always giving me book chapter and verse over and over again, even when there were times when I didn't want to hear it anymore because of the pain I was experiencing in life. She would not let up she kept reminding me that I can do all things through Christ that strengthen me. Don't let the terminator take you out. (Satan) in spite of what she was going through herself she kept telling me this.

My sister Hazel for her "statement" it gave me in site to take another look at why things happen to you. "Girl hang on in there I could have never gone through this first! God allows other people to go through things first she said in order for others to watch and learn so when there trials come they want fall apart or depart from the faith. You are strong you can do it. We all are going through something and sometimes we can't help each other all we can do is pray.

My granddaughter Tiandra for always writing me little notes of encouragement hugs and kisses and prayers. She would say Grandma Cathy let's just laugh and not worry about uncle Mont God will take care of him. We need to stick to our agenda pray, eat, sing, read, take a nap wake up and have some more fun. Out of the mouth of babes comes wisdom!

Special acknowledgements to all the people who have encouraged me over the years, all of my ladies retreat sisters and my brothers and sisters in Christ.

Introduction-Dedication

I was compelled to write this book based on the poem I wrote called a mother's silent cry. It expresses pain, emptiness, memories, losing sight and wasted time. I'm hoping that it will encourage you to cry out and speak out. In order to free yourself from holding things inside and to let them go.

My heart goes out to all the mothers out there who have been crying out and feeling as though they are not being heard. I speak out for those who have been so afraid and too embarrassed to speak out. I speak out for you, just hold on God hears your cry; I too am one of those mothers that cried out and as I tell this story I hope that you will find comfort in knowing that God hears your cry and you are not alone.

A Mother's Silent Cry

As I stood there in silence remembering the things that use to be, I tried to erase the memories hoping this would set me free. The pain it caused, the sleepless nights I embraced, and the endless tears on my face as I felt so much disgrace. Time went by day by day, night by night as I begin to lose sight. The strain on my mind with all the wasted time, I listened for my screams from all the bad dreams, but I was not relieved the emptiness as I wanted to die, and all I received was a mother's silent cry.

How many times have you found yourself standing in silence? Looking back on the things that have happened to you. Trying to forget and erase all the memories. Experiencing pain and not being able to sleep, crying for days and nights feeling like it will never end. Losing sight of everything, and not sleeping screaming, and having bad dreams night after night. Not getting any relief and feeling like you just wanted to give up and die. Then you wake up and think about all the valuable time you have wasted.

Don't give up God hears your cry and help is on the way you have just began to come out of the trance you were in and begin to fight.

About the Author

Cathy Holmes is a native of Wingate North Carolina; she is the fourth of eight children born to Fred and Arbutus Simpson. She spent most of her life in New York City where she retired from the NYC Department of Transportation. She presently resides in Forest City North Carolina with her husband Yalma. She is a loving wife, mother, a grandmother and a great-grandmother.

Cathy began writing poetry and skits, which she performed at family gathering at church as well as many other functions.

She wrote a mother's silent cry in 2005 which won her the Editor's Choice Award, and also it's recorded on a CD called the sound of poetry. She is a Distinguished member of the International Society of Poets. Some of her poems have received blue ribbon awards at cultural arts events, senior citizen centers, and Ladies Retreats.

Courage

Courage is so important when you are going through something even though you may feel all hope is lost.

Courage is taking a stand putting one foot in front of the other, stoping in your tracks and no matter what happens you take a stand.

Courage makes a statement and it lasts forever, it sends out a message for the future of all.

It has no fear and it does not fall apart it is even spoken for by others who cannot express themselves.

Courage is bravery and it is sharp and sometimes painless and painful.

Courage pulls things together in a unique way and to obtain courage we need to pray.

Courage will separate you from people who do not want you to speak out; and at times you will stand alone.

Once you exercise courage you will see change, but remember you must be strong for it is a lonely road.

It is hard for me to think of courage, and not use these words.

Come

Out

Undefeated

Remembering

Always

God is

Everlasting!

A Mother's Silent Cry

I have had many struggles and disappointments in my life from a very young age. Some of the childhood experiences I tried to pretend they were dreams, and not real. The pretense only works temporary; as you grow up they grow with you in your mind.

It is sometimes difficult to except and you find yourself talking around them, and pretending that it's someone else. I kept things inside that needed to come out; I smiled when I was crying inside.

I found myself wanting to save everyone that may have experienced anything bad that I had gone through to help free them.

I can only talk about some of my cries because I have too many stories to tell and it would be too lengthy that it would be several books so I will name a few.

I cried out when my mother died in my arms at the age of 41yrs old. To fill that emptiness, and erase the memories of losing her I sent her on a beautiful vacation, hoping one day she would return.

I was very angry, hurt, lonely, and felt as though a piece of me was ripped out torn to pieces and gone forever. I could not help save her and so I refused to accept the fact that she was really gone.

When you lose someone at a young age the fear that comes over you is unbearable at times.

Your emotions begin to build up inside, but you know in spite of that you have to fight to survive what happened. I cried out when I felt obligated to play the role of my mother after her death, caring for my siblings and trying to deal with a father that tried to escape reality by drinking.

I cried out in my dreams with memories of abuse with my flesh being fondled and my self-esteem being torn apart. I cried out as a young unwed mother struggling to care for her children when society was trying to rip my mind apart, for the wrong that they thought I had done. I cried out when I received a phone call that my sixteen year old son was on national television arrested, hand cuffed and thrown into a police van.

I cried out when I felt like the court house had become my home and all of the humiliation I received to try to make me feel like I was a criminal.

I cried out when I went to visit my son in prison and was patted down and searched and waited in the cold so long and told in so many words don't waste your time coming to see him.

I cried out when people would say if it were my son I would not go see him or send him anything, remember society says guilty as charged throw away the key.

I can go on and on about my cries because I continue to cry out but let's talk about some of your cries.

I know it's a lot of mothers out there that have cried out for something and are still crying out hold on and just remember to put your trust in God. See if you can't recognize some of their cries and if you can understand what they are going through.

A mother cries out so many times for so many reasons not all of her cries are filled with sadness some are joyful cries.

When her children grow up and leave home and go off to college and make wonderful accomplishments, and when they get married she's overwhelmed with tears of joy.

Only a mother that has experienced this will know why it becomes a mother's silent cry, her tears may roll down her face but her soul is full of joy.

When a mothers silent cry is brought on by sadness and heart ache, the feeling is so intense that the pain penetrates and pierces her heart and she sometimes because numb. The tears roll down her face without any force as she awakened in the morning only to find her pillow soaked with tears feeling totally exhausted and the cycle starts all over again.

The feeling is strong and painful and she is never the same after each event it feels unbearable she continues to be fearful that no one understands what she is going through, no one hears her and no one cares she feels like she is the only one in the world going through this.

Mothers are crying out because their children are being murdered, kidnapped sold into sex trafficking, pornography and missing in action.

Mothers are crying out from being raped and the pain from holding on to the secret is so intense that every time they hear the word or see something similar on television they are reminded about their experience and they relive it over and over again and trying to wash themselves clean hoping to remove the dirt that he left behind.

Mothers are crying out from being used or deceived in a relationship their dream of being married to someone they love so much had been shattered when he married another woman. They felt like their world has been turned upside down making her feel less than a woman because she felt like she had been replaced.

Mothers are crying out because they have been married to someone for many years thinking they have such a wonderful marriage only to find out about the dirty little secrets that everyone knew about but them. He has more children, he has been cheating on me with another women and she's pregnant.

Mothers are crying out from being sexually abused as well as physically and mentally some are being tortured locked in the closet burned with cigarettes, punched and beaten broken ribs, yet they cry out inside but they continue to stay in that relationship. They think its love but what does love have to do with that! Her cry is smothered in silence in fear of her children hearing her screams as she is trying to protect them. Some Mothers are crying out they have been shot stabbed tied up locked in closets and basements feed drugs and forced to sell their bodies. They cry out and feel they have no hope and no courage they become helpless.

Mothers cry out when they have carried a child for nine months and are being robbed cursed out some have even been struck down and are afraid of their own children.

I cry out and I shout out hold on don't let go God has delivered me and I know he can deliver you he does not lie and his love endureth forever. He made the greatest sacrifice he has ever made when he gave his only son.

Mothers I cry out to you, you are special beautiful and I urge you to be strong you take on so many roles in life there is a Queen in you screaming out loud, and its time to let her come out. Don't allow yourself to be destroyed by Satan's devises life is to short not to make the best of it.

I encourage you don't let your inspirations dreams and visions for life go to waste because of what has happened to you. "Fight the devil wants you stopped in your tracks he wants you to give up all hope when there is still hope.

I cry out to all the mothers out there your struggle may seem too great to bare but don't give up the fight.

Mothers are crying out all over the world in reference to some of these events that have occurred in their life.

The Telephone Call

I have seen the movie 48 hours many times but I never dreamed that my son would be playing a role in that movie in real life they whispered on the phone into my ears "Your son is chained inside a bus traveling cross country to prison". The language was strange to me he talked about the system but I didn't have a clue what central booking was. He talked non -stop without any room for questions and then the phone went click. Just that quick there was silence again I began to cry out in the middle of the night tears just ran down my face. I buried myself into my pillow screaming in silence and my mind became scrambled with racing thoughts.

It was such a strain on my mind I knew that I had to find courage and hold on to it and I could not waste another moment of time because I was beginning to lose sight.

I began to scream out like the sound of thunder during a rain storm it felt as though the sound was being pulled from my stomach through my mouth yet it was silent.

You began to think about all the mothers that had experienced being awakened up in the middle of the night with a phone call like this what in the world could have been going through their minds.

I grabbed a hold of myself and concentrated on prayer and talked inside discussing the strength that I needed to go through what was happening to me.

The only thing left to do was to wait scriptures came to my mind like bolts of lightning. One was "Trust in the Lord with all your heart and lean not to your own understanding".

In spite of my flesh trying to fight against the spirit I was reminded that I could do all things through Christ that strengthens me.

I was tired and exhausted like a child that had been running around all day and had fell asleep before you could finish a bed time story.

The burden was so heavy that I felt disconnected from my body I didn't even remember when my mind decided to rest for the night, because I had cried out for so long.

When morning came my pillow was soaked as if someone had poured a cup of water on it all I could say was thank you lord for allowing me to see a new day.

Missing In Action

Do you remember the movie "Missing in Action"? Could you imagine how you would feel if someone in your family went missing.

I would hear this on the news and the thought of it made me quiver and now to think it actually happened to me.

Some of us make comments about if it ever happened to me I would.........................Stop right there, you really don't have a clue what you would do or how you would react.

Let me explain to you about when my mother died in my arms I was silent but I was screaming so hard inside. So when my child went missing I screamed out so loud Lord where could he be? Is he dead? I thought the worst first as most of us mothers do we allow our mental mind to kick in first. Was he kidnapped? Was he in an accident? Racing thoughts start coming from everywhere.

I began to torment myself for days I even began to question God, Why is this happening? I lost all my focused I could not remember that the same God that has brought me this far and said he will never leave me nor forsake me is the same God that will see me through this.

I began to drift back into my own thoughts disregarding the word of God completely. In spite of this I was reminded so many times to trust God he is still good no matter what was happening in my life.

The flesh was fighting against my spirit so therefore it was not registering. I was not resisting the devil and he was literally tearing my mind apart some days I allowed him to distract me, and it took my focus off the word of God.

I was not able to think just act on impulses, and when you allow that to happen to you believe me you are not focused. I found that I allowed my mind to go on auto pilot and nothing else seemed to be working.

I totally lost control and began to take matters into my own hands I remember going to work and making flyers of my sons picture and the sign read "Missing in action have you seen this child please call this number you may be saving this child's life.

I even put the police department's number on the flyer for the contact number I proceeded to walk blocks and blocks posting flyers. In desperation that someone would help me find my child. As I walked I cried and cried questioning people along the way with no response.

The following day I woke up and found myself physically and mentally exhausted and then I began to get angry. I thought for a moment how foolish this is and also how dangerous it was I said to myself I can't do this again but that only lasted for a moment.

I got my sister involved to go on the mad hunt again, I decided to drive this time we cried together and talked about the situation. We went to the most dangerous neighborhoods searching not even realizing it. Then I started to feel so bad allowing her to go with me. Thinking about the things family will do for you out of love and concern.

We both came to ourselves for a moment and stated to pray. I promised I would not do this again and leave it in the hands of the lord. When you let the devil ride you like a roller coaster you will end up lying to yourself because that lasted for a few days and I was off on the search again. I went alone this time because I decided not to involve my family in this dangerous foolishness anymore.

I went to work every day trying to smile it was very stressful and mind draining on the job not knowing where my child was or how he was doing.

The pain from that experience was so intense and it felt so unbearable, in spite of it all the thoughts raced through my head that God will not put any more on you than you can bare.

I was tired and physically, mentally and emotionally worn out, I stopped and began to pray yet still crying and I refused to give up my search. One day the search ended he surfaced.

Whatever Happened To My Gifted Child?

I sat on my bed one rainy day tears running from my eyes and thoughts bouncing everywhere as if they could fly right out of the top of my head.

I had a gifted child and it seems as though he allowed his gift to be snatched away from him in a split second.

Question does your child appear to be the same in your presence? Or can you be so blind that you don't really know what's going on.

That's some of the things society speaks about, I heard parents speak about their children and the things they used to find in their rooms. It may seem unbelievable until your own nightmare appears.

If you began to experience a horrible feeling that comes over you and the lack of trust is driven from you day by day, this is a mother's rude awakening and you began to question what happened where did I go wrong?

The thought of what will people say? The shame, the embarrassment and finally where is this going to lead?

One day you are crushed the next day you fight back, the people you thought you could trust turns there back on you at the very time that you think you need them.

Watch out you may become an outcast you are labeled and the whispers began to start. Talking about things they know nothing about.

While you are still left with the question what ever happened to my gifted child? You need support you need a hug but you feel like you have been stomped in the mud and stabbed in the back. Some family members began to question you in disbelief as though the problem was created by you.

Hold on tight this is how Satan operates he wants you destroyed especially while you are hurting and vulnerable he wants to kill you while you are down.

The Warning "Beware"

Remember the devil will use anyone and anything to get to you, take time out to pray so you can think with a clear head. You are going through something and sometimes everyone does, not know how to assist you in a crisis. Watch whose shoulder you cry on because some people will cause you to have more pain, be careful take time out to pray continuously stay close to God and don't pull back from him in time of trouble, that's when you need him more.

Mothers that are crying out today and searching for answers as to why this is happening to them hold your head up God has a plan for us all he is a deliverer and his grace and mercy is everlasting.

I want to share some more of my poems that have been written over the years to comfort and encourage the readers.

A Cry Out for "Ma "Ma

I cry out for all the mothers in the world
that are not being treated right

I know how lonely and painful it is not to feel loved

When you have brought a child into this world and
they can't even find the time to call and say I love you

Mothers don't ask for much you "see" they just
want to hear a voice, receive a card that they can
keep forever and a memory they can hold on to

I think a mother deserves much more than that, "but" if
you can't do anything else make sure you show her love

A cry out for "Ma "Ma

Remember if you are not showing her anything
now, when she is gone you might cry out
for "Ma "Ma but it will be too late.

It's hard to show someone something
when they are not around

You may know someone that this poem is writing about
comfort them by reaching out and letting them know to
hold on just a little while longer. Leave this thing in his
hands and he will see you through.

"Ma "Ma we need to talk

"Ma "Ma we I wish you were still here we need to talk

I need feedback from you because you understood

This world is trying to swallow me up and spit me out

You are not here to tell me how to handle my battles

"Ma "Ma I wish you were still here we need to talk

I cry sometimes when I reach out
to you and you are not here

I have so much fear because I remember how much I

Loved you and how you were always near

"Ma "Ma I wish you were still here we need to talk

I need to hold your hand and go for a walk

I need to hear you say everything is going to be alright

I need to buy you some flowers, wish
you a happy mother's day

Say how much I love you and make your day bright

"Ma "Ma we need to talk

I want to remind everyone out there that are still enjoying their mother,

Embrace her and treat her good while she is still in sight, show love while they live and you will have great memories when they are gone.

I wrote this poem on behalf of a mother that was dying and she longed to see her son. I cry out and shout out to children don't wait until it's too late to reach out for "Ma "Ma.

My Child are you there?

My child I long to see you for days, months, and years

I look for you in the sunset, and glance
for you when the wind blows

I feel your presence near my bedside
as my life ponders away

I long to talk, walk, and hold your
hand along the passing day

My life is almost over and I didn't
have much time with you

Now yesterday is gone and tomorrow may never be mine

And when I think of the passing moments

I ask myself my child are you there?

Life is too short so don't waste valuable time, spend more time loving, encouraging, uplifting, and helping one another. Find some time to communicate, and sit a while. Make memories that would be worth a life time that's what life is all about.

When I wrote a mother's silent cry I had so many things going on in my life, the trials and tribulations that were taking place I felt were too much to bear.

I began to sit down and examine myself after reading the end of the poem which reads..... All I received is a mothers silent cry I have to intrepid it for the readers.

When you are going through a storm in life and you feel there is no way out, stop and turn it over to God he already has it worked out.

I wanted a happy ending but at the time it was not happening so I paused and said all I received was a mother's silent cry.... Meaning pain, heartache, and disappointment. Not realizing at the time that I left God out of the plan he knew how the story would end. He has a way of leaving everything the same but yet he changes the way you look at it. He gives you that peace you need to get through it all.

I cry out to you don't try to figure out anything he needs to be the center of your life and he will work it out for good!

So if you are out there holding everything in experiencing all the heavy weight on your shoulders trying to cover up all the horrible things you have experienced in life. Feeling pain, disgrace wrapped around you pride holding you down, and feeling emptiness and wasting all of life's valuable time.

I urge you to stop take a closer look and turn it over to God don't give up no matter what you are going through he hears your cry.

Turn all that energy you are using from negative to positive take the focus off you, start thinking about how you can help somebody that may be experiencing the worse things in life.

Show love spread encouragement, embrace your fears and stop worrying about how your story will end.

I hope I have captivated your heart through reading of this book and inspired you to have courage and share your experiences with others.

I know as I continue this journey in life there will be a mother's silent cry part two.

Tributes to the Writer

As I cared for my sister Peggy during her illness and because of her stroke she wasn't able to express herself I would write and she would say I like that for you I wish I could go head. She was proud of me and loved me very much, she posted my picture everywhere if she seen an article about me in the paper. She cried out Cathy you know my story and I spoke for her. She wanted me to write a poem for her I sit down with her and threw out something's and she would say yes like that when I was finished she said you alright you know what happened.

Speak for me

I want to tell you so many things I want to remind
you about my wonderful dreams I sit and listen to
everyone wanting to respond but I can't so I don't
have much fun I want to hold and touch someone
create a life get married and really bond the days go
by so fast I want to cry but when I think about how
blessed I am I just sit and sigh I continue to listen
and not to speak I continue to grow strong and not

to be weak and because of the faith and hope I have
I know one day I'll be in Gods bosom fast asleep!

My sister Cathy has always been a very loving and caring person which made it easy for her to take on the role of caring for her three sisters and one brother that was left at home when our mother died. Cathy was only seventeen years old when our mother died yet she unselfishly gave up her childhood for the good of her siblings thanks to her love and dedication we stayed together until we grew up.

She has always been a hard worker which led to her career with the City of New York and also as the president of one of the city's largest union. After her retirement nothing stopped her she relocated became a Hospice Volunteer, a Community Worker, the ECA Club and County President and then the District President. Her greatest works are those she does for the lord a proud member of the Church of Christ she has truly exemplified the spirit of Christ in loving and caring for others. Was the Willing Workers President and has taught many bible classes, spoke at ladies retreats, a ladies day coordinator and a anything you need me to do worker.

She has always been a writer, skits, poems and plays though she has faced many disappointments and struggles in life none of these things have moved her. She is still determined to trust in the lord, because she realizes that through it all the lord delivered her. So as she shares her story of a mother's pain as she dealt with her sons ordeal. She has come through the fire and now the beautiful Christian that God has brought fourth is a blessing to all.

I love her dearly she is my biological sister who took on the role of my mother and now she is my sister in Christ and my best friend. She has truly been a blessing to my life and may God continue to bless her and grant her the desires of her heart.

Love,

Rosa